Wishes Before Midnight

AN ANTHOLOGY OF POEMS & SHORT STORIES IN ENGLISH AND FRENCH

by Fayruz Mandil

Cedar Rose Publications

First published by Cedar Rose Publications, 2020

Cedar Rose Publications
3003 Bern
Switzerland

ISBN 978-2-8399-3118-2

A CIP catalogue record for this book is available from the National Library of Switzerland.

Cover image by: ©Abby Mansfield
Layout design by: Divya Venkatesh

I would like to express my eternal thanks and gratitude to my friends and illustrators Ada Basford, Marie Kolly, Abby Mansfield, Lauren Papot, Nina Taniguchi, Chisa Togo, and Divya Venkatesh for their advice, collaboration, and for putting their heart into their beautiful artwork.

With love, this book is dedicated to my illustrators, to my siblings Mohammed, Basil, and Samira Mandil, and to my parents, Salah Mandil, and Salha Elkurdi.

© Nina Taniguchi

SUMMER IN VENICE

3,000 euros. Celeste closed her eyes and attempted some mental arithmetic. That was more than twice her monthly rent, which she still found overpriced. She winced, remembering her gloomy mood every time she transferred her hard-earned money to her landlord's account. There went her precious 1,500 euros every first of the month. But she could not deny how much she loved her little studio with its rusty Juliet balcony in the middle of nowhere Haute-Savoie.

3,000 euros. That covered about half a year in Vanuatu. She chuckled softly. Her friends Denise and Mariam would have picked up on the reference and laughed too. It is funny how often the trio of friends compared value for money anywhere but in their country when they knew, deep down in their hearts, that their hometown was someone else's paradise.

3,000 euros. And that did not even cover everything in the course. At least she had her own room with its private en-suite bathroom. The view from her room was not what she would call spectacular, but the hostel's location was decent. If 3,000 euros was the cost of a treat to herself, so be it. God knew what a horrible year she had. But who, if they were truly honest with themselves, did not dream of going to an art retreat? And in Venice! She lost count of how many negative comments were made when she told her friends and colleagues that she was spending her summer in the Venetian city; 'But it smells awful!', 'It's SO expensive though!', 'Why? It's SO touristy!' Bla Bla Bla. But Celeste was wise enough to know that the very people who are so ready to criticize are the most envious.

Celeste knew that being in Venice this summer was somehow her destiny. Countless times her mother told her how she chose to name her Celeste because 'because she is a star and destined for great things.' How silly, thought Celeste. And that name. Bleurgh! But over the years, Celeste had come to like her mother's story and, eventually, her name too.

'Celeste, are you listening?' Celeste immediately snapped out of her reverie and nodded her head furiously. Giovanna gave Celeste an unconvinced look before resuming her lecture.

Giovanna was her mentor for the summer. Celeste found that her mentor's name could not be more Italian nor could her looks. She was rather petite, with long sleek chestnut brown hair, heavy makeup and an impeccable French manicure. How on earth Giovanna managed to keep her nails so clean while working with paint was beyond her. Celeste could sense that Giovanna was a no-nonsense person but she found her warm too, with a charming accent. Italian is definitely a beautiful language, thought Celeste. It is not just its musicality. It has emotions too, like every uttered word is the most significant thing to ever be said. She nearly let out an 'awww' the other day when asking what is a *pizza bianco* and the pizzaiolo answered "ehh focaccia with olive oiiil and a little beet of salteee."

But Celeste was not in Venice to swoon over the Italians' accents or their food. She was here to improve her artistic skills and quickly. It was already Day 5 of her art retreat and today the attendees were to walk in the extremely narrow alleys of Venice, look up in the direction of the sky and sketch the locals' laundry drying above their heads.

'No pencil and no eraser!' ordered Giovanna. 'Only a paintbrush and watercolour!' Well thank god this is not graded, thought Celeste. She took a glimpse at the watercolour palette. It was Sennelier1887's latest pastel edition. Gorgeous. With just the right amount of water, one can create a beautiful gradient on their canvas.

With the world going through one of the worst financial recessions in history, Celeste was surprised to see so many tourists out and about. Venice in the summer was especially packed, and while Celeste loved the sun and heat, she knew some people would find them unbearable. So what should have taken ten minutes to walk to really took about forty. Celeste and her troop stopped at a sunlit alley as Giovanna wanted them to practice their shading. 'Okay *ragazzi*. Pick one or two clothes hanging above your head and paint them. Remember, no pencil or eraser!'

Celeste loved shades of blue and grey, so she was looking up, in the endless, entangled clothing lines, for a white dress and perhaps a pair of denim to sketch. Wow, this is hard thought Celeste. She was particularly good at observational drawing, but it was one thing to sit comfortably and draw an object in front of you, and another thing to stand while holding a sketchbook in one hand and a paintbrush in the other. There was a bit of a breeze rustling the clothes, but perhaps that inspired Celeste to add motion to her sketches.

She was enjoying herself, lost in the *mondo* of Venice, when 'Oh my god! You are SO detailed! How can you sketch like this? I would just die! Ugh.

I'm keeping mine simple.' Celeste turned her head to the obnoxious voice addressing her. She was a tall, horribly dressed blonde woman, probably in her forties. She had a familiar accent but Celeste couldn't place where it was from.

'Where did you say you are from?' asked Celeste.

'Cologne. Why?'

Ah yes, THAT place, smiled Celeste in recognition. 'Nothing. Just asking.' (But she wasn't really). She stole a glance at Ms Deutschland's sketches. Lame.

Celeste almost challenged Ms Deutschland with a witty comeback when Giovanna suddenly appeared behind her.

'*Ché bello, Celeste.*' (Take that, Ms Deutschland).

'*Ma forse prova piu ombreggiatura su questio lato del tuo schizzo?*'

Celeste wasn't sure why Giovanna assumed she speaks Italian, but with her fluency in French and Spanish, she could get by. Celeste took the opportunity to step away from Ms Obnoxious and stand closer to Giovanna instead. At least Giovanna wouldn't be making such petty remarks.

Celeste gently moved her sleeve to check the time. It was 6 o'clock. *L'ora dell'aperitivo.* And time to head back to the hostel. Despite the heat and the crowd, it had been a beautiful day. The sun was closer to the canals now, illuminating the Venitian city. This was Instagrammers' o'clock. An instamoment.

Back at their dorms, Celeste and the crew had some time to freshen up and Celeste wanted to change outfits. It was Italy after all, and presentation mattered here. They sure loved black and their leather here in Italy, but Celeste knew white, or off-white, was trendy too. She showered and put on her cream lace dress she bought before the trip, her Marciano ballerinas, and her black Prada aviators. She sensed it was going to be a special night on the town and couldn't wait for more Venetian adventures.

© Fayruz Mandil

ALICE RETOLD

After checking the weather an uncountable number of times since sunrise this morning, a ray of sunlight was finally making its way through the curtains. Alice jumped out of the nook, feeling excited. Finally, after what she thought was a monsoonal summer, they deserved sunnier days.

'Lorna! Lorna! Lorna!' Alice was trying to get her older sister's attention, whose eyes seemed glued to her phone, all day and all night.

'Millennials' she once heard her Aunt Julie say, and when Alice figured out what it meant, she smirked cheekily.

'Whaaaat?' answered Lorna, clearly annoyed by the disturbance.

'Can we go outside? It's really sunny!' pleaded Alice.

'Ugh, really?' Lorna had to roll her eyes for added effects.

'Come on! You promised Mum and Dad that we would do something together.'

'Okay fine. Maybe I'll get tanned.'

They lived quite far out in the countryside, just some minutes away from public parks and woodlands. As the sisters walked further into the woods, the sights and scents made Alice want to explore. But instead, Lorna took out her earphones and sat under a large oak tree, and with the sun shining so brightly, a gigantic spot of shade was forming on the ground. So much for tanning, thought Alice.

'Lorna, do you want to walk some more and explore?'

'Not really. I just want to sit and chill.'

What was the point of going out in nature, in the fresh air, to stare at your phone, when you could stay indoors and do that? Nevermind her, thought Alice. She decided to explore on her own.

As she walked, Alice wished her sister had come along and given the place a chance. It was beautiful; sprawling green grass, birds singing, the wind whistling softly. Suddenly, she spotted animal tracks. Deer's?

Badgers'? Hares'? She spotted a few of these before, some feet away from her backyard. She wondered where the tracks would lead to. Hopefully nowhere dangerous? After all, curiosity killed the cat.

As Alice plodded deeper into the woods, she felt the temperature drop. The ground felt softer, cushioned by layer upon layer of fallen young twigs and leaves. Every now and then, she felt something bouncy under her feet when she realised that she was walking on large, colourful mushrooms, ranging from scarlet red to indigo blue. She was completely spellbound.

Lost in a dreamery, Alice spotted another large tree, but the trunk of this one looked like a door. She frowned slightly, to see better. It was a door! And it had a knob. Was it someone's home? She approached the tree cautiously, leaned her head against it to hear if there was anything inside it. Nothing. But a small text was encrypted on the copper-coloured knob: 'I took the road less travelled by and that made all the difference.' Robert Frost. She knew his poetry all too well. But what did all this mean? Is she meant to open the door? Feeling intrigued, she turned the knob clockwise. The door opened, and Alice took one small step forward before she fell.

She fell into a big black tunnel of nothingness. She wasn't screaming but her heart was pounding. Where was this endless black tunnel taking her?

What felt like light years later, Alice landed on a patch of what felt like new green grass. She looked up and found the same oak tree from the woods standing in front of her. However, this time the tree had colourful objects hanging from its branches. She frowned. Where was she?

Feeling lightheaded, she got up, making her way towards the tree. When she was close enough to see what was hanging from the branches, she gasped.

Hundreds of origamis, books, pencils, cups and spoons of all colours were tied to equally colourful ropes hanging from the tree. But this wasn't all. There were books hanging too, all those that she had read and loved so much. She wanted to grab them all but felt this could be a trap. She lifted her head, looking higher into the foliage, looking for a clue.

In the heart of the impressive crown of green leaves, Alice spotted a purple rope of which hung a greeting card that said 'Read me'. This must be it, thought Alice. But how to get there? She was good at many things, but climbing trees wasn't one of them. I must try, thought Alice. There was one branch to her right that stooped a bit lower than her eye level. If she jumped high enough....and she did, without looking down or imagining herself trip into one nasty fall.

She could finally reach the greeting card and was surprised by its coarse texture. She opened it and it read: 'This is a riddle game and your way back home. Find every greeting card with a 'Quote Me' embossed on them, read the instructions and answer the riddles. If you answer them all correctly, we will open the door for you.'

Alice was completely bewildered. This couldn't be real nor really happening. This eerie woodland was probably the most beautiful place she's ever seen. And she loved riddles. She started searching deeper in the leafage for any greeting cards that would show themselves. She spotted one, grabbed it with both hands, and with her heart in her mouth, read aloud: 'Who said: 'If I had my mouth, I would bite?' She knew this one. It was one of her favourites. So she answered, aloud and enunciating every letter: 'Don John in 'Much Ado About Nothing' by William Shakespeare.' The greeting card then slowly turned into an Edelweiss flower before vanishing with a little 'poof'. How many more of these riddles, wondered Alice.

She found another card, this time right above her head: 'From which novel is the following quote from: 'There are only the pursued, the pursuing, the busy and the tired?' That's a memorable one, remembered Alice before loudly, and once again exaggeratingly enunciating every word, uttering: 'From 'The Great Gatsby' by F. Scott Fitzerland.'

And so it went - Alice was tested on her literary knowledge and her memory, until ninety-nine quotes later, she heard a door open softly. Alice looked down and saw that the way out was open and she had won the riddle game. Standing on a narrow branch and trying to keep her balance, Alice jumped to the ground, landing perfectly on her feet.

She bent forward, as the door was small, walked into the unknown, hoping it would be her way home, when 'Alice! Alice! Can you hear me? Alice!' It was Lorna's voice and she sounded worried.

'Mmm. Ooof. My head! Where am I? What happened?'

'What do you mean 'Where am I?' We're in the park and we need to get out of here right now!' shouted Lorna.

'Why? What happened?' asked Alice, her head still spinning.

'It's those mushrooms. They give off a powder that can be toxic and if it is inhaled for too long, spells you into a long, psychedelic dream. I'm guessing you had one of those?'

'How do you know this? I thought you hated Biology class with Ms Augustin.'

'I do. But one time we learned about those mushrooms in class and for once the lesson wasn't boring, so I listened. Come on Alice, let's go. We don't want to fall into another one of those dreams, do we?'

Drowsily, Alice stood up and followed her sister, who was still holding her phone in her hand.

Alice turned her head and took one last look at the woods. The animal tracks were still there.

© Lauren Papot

TERMINAL 5

Nadia was on a high. She's been looking forward to the conference for weeks, organising and preparing herself down to the smallest detail - what she'll wear, how she'll begin her workshop, who she'll try to meet. Exciting times indeed.

And on top of all that, she gets to travel to Singapore for the very first time. Ever since she watched 'Crazy Rich Asians', she imagined the Singaporean food, the nightlife, the technology. She just couldn't wait.

She was sitting in Terminal Five, waiting for boarding at Gate 25. She always loved airports - such fascinating places and, often, shopping tax free was heaven. But she was feeling tired now, and anxious to get on the plane. She took out her phone, looking again at the conference's website. Genius event management team whoever they were, thought Nadia. Gardens by the Bay was the main venue, with breakfast and coffee breaks in the Orchids Garden, and happy hour at Tiare, the rooftop terrace and pool, overlooking the bay and the hustle and bustle of the city-nation. Her workshop was in the Flower Dome, the one that she got selected to lead. Finally, after all her years of hard work and being taken for granted, Nadia secured the position of a workshop leader in botanical conservation. It may only be a temporary position lasting around a week, but it meant the world to her.

Still staring at her phone screen and smiling goofily at the conference's programme, she perked when hearing a voice that sounded familiar to her. Too familiar. She looked up. It couldn't be. It was Rachel Eingrennemann, her former boss and witch of a woman. Oh no. Please don't spot me, please don't spot me, prayed Nadia. Too late.

'Nadia ElHalawi! Is that you?' Oh crap.

'Hi Rachel! Oh my god, it's been years! How have you been? What are you doing here?' Nadia exclaimed with as much pretense as she could pull.

'Going to the 2020 Conservation Conference of course' answered Rachel in a tone that implied how obvious was the response.

'Of course' answered Nadia, hoping she didn't sound too bitter or sarcastic. 'That's so great!'

'Well, it looks like you're going too' replied Rachel, nosely looking at the conference brochures and boarding pass sticking out of Nadia's travel bag.

'Yes I am. I'm so excited.'

'I'd love to catch up, Nadia. Where are you sitting?'

'4A.'

'Oh. You're in First Class?'

'I am. My employer made the booking for me.'

'Really? And who might that be?' asked Rachel, eyebrows raised in surprise.

'Gardenia Conservation International. I'm leading the workshop on botanical conservation.'

'Wow.'

'Yeah, I'm so thrilled.' Nadia then noticed, though the tension between them was still there, she was no longer afraid of Rachel nor hated her. Rather, she felt sorry for her. But Nadia worked hard for this and she was going to enjoy the fruits of her labour.

'Oh. They're calling for First Class passengers. Sorry Rachel. See you at the conference?'

But they weren't calling for boarding. Nadia had to think of something to say. Sensing Rachel's eyes on her as she walked away, she ran to the ladies room. She couldn't face Rachel right now. How unbelievable, to bump into her here of all places, thought Nadia. She opened the door of the ladies room slightly, feeling awkward while other women going in and out of the room were giving her odd looks.

Acting like a spy, Nadia looked left and right for any signs of Rachel. She was nowhere to be seen. Phew. The coast was clear. She glanced at the announcement board. No sign of boarding anytime soon and her flight was delayed. Great. Time for a coffee I guess, thought Nadia.

She walked past several gates in Terminal Five, looking for a decent coffee house. A neon sign that read "Coffeed Up" was blindly illuminating. Nadia noticed the long line of customers waiting to order, but she knew the brand and taste of their coffee well enough to spare her patience.

Thinking about what to order, the conference, Singapore, her ex-boss, Nadia was lost in her thoughts. She jumped when she felt a tap on her shoulder. Cautiously, Nadia turned around and came face-to-face with a Punjabi looking woman, probably in her fifties. The lady was crying and her eyes were red. Really red. She was sniffling and holding an obviously overused tissue paper.

'Sorry Miss. I really need the bathroom, my bag is heavy and I've been queuing for a while now. Do you think you can look after my bag while I go to the bathroom please?'

Nadia felt conflicted. This was a complete stranger and she had no idea what the lady had in her bag. Nadia studied the woman's face. She seemed kind and had the look of someone who recently received bad news. Nadia knew that look.

'Ummm. Sure' Nadia finally responded.

'Thank you. You're too kind' replied the sad lady before she ran to the ladies room.

Nadia wondered what was wrong with her. And where was she heading? Why was she alone? It felt like a while had passed when Nadia saw her coming out of the ladies room. She had brushed her hair, applied some face powder, and as far as Nadia could see, she wasn't crying anymore. The lady spotted Nadia looking and smiled. Nadia smiled back.

'Thank you Miss' said the lady.

'No worries' answered Nadia, a bit shyly. The lady was looking at her rather curiously but Nadia pretended not to notice.

'I'm Salma' said the lady, before offering her hand.

Nadia hesitated until she too offered her hand and said 'Nice to meet you. I'm Nadia.'

They were getting close to the counter when Salma asked 'What would you like Nadia?'

'Oh no, it's okay, thank you' answered Nadia shyly, realising Salma was offering to pay.

'No please, I insist' said Salma.

'Okay. Thanks. A Cappuccino, please. Thanks a lot.'

'Of course. Why don't you take a seat and then I'll join you?'

Salma clearly longed for company, for someone to talk to. Understandable really. But Nadia was a nervous traveller and did not want to lose track of time. Also, she didn't want to be rude.

'Okay, sure. I'll see you inside?'

'Yes, see you in a bit.'

Nadia looked for a table by the window where she could watch the planes taking off and landing. She could also see an announcement board close to the window and keep a close eye on it.

Some minutes later, Salma met her at the table, carrying an Americano and a Cappuccino on a small tray.

While Salma was settling into her seat, she started making small talk.

'So tell me Nadia, where are you heading?'

'Singapore. And you?'

'Karachi' answered Salma rather blandly.

'Are you visiting your family?'

'No. My brother passed away and I'm going to his funeral.'

There was a moment of silence. Nadia felt so guilty and awkward, when finally she had the courage to speak 'Oh my goodness. I'm so sorry. I didn't mean to pry.'

'No it's okay. You didn't know. But let's talk about you. What are you travelling to Singapore for?'

'I'm going to a big conference on environmental conservation and I'll be leading a workshop on botanical conservation. I'm so excited.' Realising she blurted out more than necessary, she blushed, feeling embarrassed.

Salma gave her that curious look again before she said 'you sound nervous.'

'Yes. Sorry. I just saw my horrible ex-boss and she's going to the conference too. Just my luck.'

'Ah, don't worry about it. Forget her' Salma shrugged it off, as if she had heard of bigger problems. She probably had.

'Where in Singapore is the conference?'

'Gardens by the Bay.'

'That's wonderful. I love Singapore.'

'Oh you been?'

'Yes, one of my closest cousins lives there. You should get in touch with her, just in case you need anything.'

'Oh thank you. That would be really nice.'

'Sure, no problem. I'll give you her number. Her name is Selina.'

Nadia's eyes sparkled. 'Really? That's my best friend's name', said Nadia with a smile. Salma smiled back warmly.

'So what's with this ex-boss of yours? What happened?'

'Oh. It's a long story. I think she's prejudiced really. And always gave me the worst tasks to do. And she kept making those mean half-jokes, you know?'

'That's awful.'

'I know.' Nadia sighed loudly.

'But you know, this so-called chance encounter with your ex-boss can't be just a coincidence.'

'What do you mean?' asked Nadia, genuinely confused.

'I mean, what if it was God's way of giving you a second chance?'

'How though?'

'Well, why don't you show her how she didn't break you? Act and dress confident, and avoid her toxicity. I'm sure there are plenty more people to impress and spend time with. It would be a shame being in such a beautiful place and worry about what an insecure person thinks of you.'

'You're right. Thank you Salma.' said Nadia, realising that this was the first time she said her name. She looked over at the announcement board hanging behind the coffee house and jumped. 'Oh! I'm so sorry. It looks like my flight is finally boarding. I better go.'

'No problem. I understand. You don't want to miss that flight! Nadia, thank you. And enjoy your conference.'

To her own surprise, Nadia got up and pulled Salma into a hug. She smelled rose water on her hair. 'Thank you, Salma. You've been very kind. I'm so sorry again for your loss. I'll be thinking of you.'

Salma gave a small smile and said 'Me too. Here, let me quickly write down Selina's phone number for you.' She grabbed a napkin from their table and scribbled hastily.

'Thank you so much. It was so nice meeting you. Have a safe flight.' She paused. 'And I wish you strength on your journey, Salma.'

'Thank you, Nadia.'

Nadia walked fast back to Gate 25. They were calling First Class passengers. She turned around and could just about make out Salma and waved her hand before showing her passport and boarding pass, taking a leap of faith and stepping inside the aircraft.

© Ada Basford

CAPPUCCINO

'Graines et Café'. Fancy name, thought Ale. He wondered why such a name? Was his native language not beautiful enough? Or did everything really sound better in French? The coffee was overpriced and overrated, and he wanted to laugh when he saw the price of the pastries. Unreal. What were they made of? Powdered gold? An instant coffee at home would have been much cheaper. But Ale didn't have time to go back to his apartment and he really wasn't in the mood to face his flatmates, not even in the daytime. But he needed something to occupy his hand, a pick-me-up to keep him going until the end of the day.

It had been a warm day, with many walks of life in summery clothes. A day like this attracted tourists like bees to honey. Ale found it amusing how many tourists would do the exact same thing: guided tour, coffee break at Starbucks, guided tour continued. But today Ale was not in the mood to be in crowded places and put on a happy face, even if, really, it was an important part of his job. Luckily his coffee breaks were long, and he had time to find some place where he could be alone.

So he walked away from the crowds, from the foreign languages, from the long lines of taxis looking like yellow caterpillars. Nothing felt far enough until he spotted 'Graines et Café'. It was so unlike him to be in such places, but today he didn't care. As soon as he walked in, this little bell above his head gave out a gentle 'ding-dong' and the staff looked up and pronounced a formal *'Buenas Tardes'*.

It was a poshier version of Starbucks but the concept was the same: order, pay, wait for your name to be called, and either take a seat or ask for a take-away. Looking at the menu, Ale sniggered at all the options with their little French names: *Cappuccino à la crème de caramel, Cappuccino au lait d'amande.* Not sure I can afford any pastry, let alone any fancy coffees, thought Ale.

'What would you like, *amigo*?' asked the equally fancy dressed barista.

'Un pequeño Cappuccino, por favor.'

'Bueno. ¿Y tu nombre?'

'Ale.'

Ale looked around the coffee house and was surprised to find it busy with both locals and tourists. Studying the place like a hawk, he almost missed the barista calling out his name. He was about to grab the cup from the counter when someone else did. He looked over. It was a 30-something year old girl. She wasn't what people might call a beauty queen but Ale found her striking. She was deeply tanned and her facial features were unique.

'Sorry Miss but I think that's my cup' said Ale, a little awkwardly.

'I don't think so. I ordered a small Cappuccino and my name is Ale' she answered in a confident tone that took him by surprise.

'Your name is Ale too? What's it short for?'

'Alexa. I think that's your order coming up.' Sure enough, it was his cup and the barista was marking 'Ale' with a big black Sharpie on it.

'You're right. I'm sorry.'

'It's fine. I better get going.'

'Sure.' Ale watched her. She didn't seem in a hurry. Was she avoiding him?

It turned out that they were walking in the same direction, back towards the centre of town, towards the heartbeat of the city.

'Sorry Alexa, I don't mean to sound like a stalker, but it looks like we're walking in the same direction. Do you mind if we walk together?'

She shrugged her shoulders before she said 'Alright.'

He wasn't sure what was so intriguing about her but he felt like talking to her. This time he studied her a bit more closely. She was wearing a long white dress shirt, buttoned at the elbows. Her tan contrasted with her silver suede shoes that matched her earrings. She had on some makeup that she hid well with her large aviators. Her hair was tied in a bun, held together by a silver scrunchie to match her shoes and jewelry. She seemed comfortable in her own skin. Why was she alone, wondered Ale.

'So what brings you to this city?' asked Ale, trying to break the ice.

'My friend from college got married a few days ago in Buena Vista and I thought I'd visit the rest of the country.'

'And what do you think of it so far?' asked Ale.

'Well actually, this is my fifth visit to this country. I love it.'

'Wow! You must know it better than me!' laughed Ale, hoping she would too. She didn't but gave him a warm smile in response.

'I doubt it. But my Spanish is improving quickly.'

'*¿En serio? Hablas español?*'

She smiled. '*Si, hace cinco años que aprendo el idioma.*'

'*¡Que padre! ¿Dónde has aprendido español?*'

'*Durante mis estudios, en la universidad.*'

'*Que bueno.* Your Spanish is great.'

Alexa blushed before she smiled and said '*Gracias.*'

'So what are you up to now?' asked Ale.

'I just finished a guided tour and I'm heading back to my hotel. And you?'

'Nothing.'

This time Alexa turned to face and look at him properly. Was she reading his mind? 'Oh. Okay. Wanna hang out?'

'Sure. Why not?' He seemed surprised by her question. 'Why don't we meet in front of your hotel and go for a walk?'

'Sounds like a plan. I'm staying at Colibri Hotel. Meet at 5?'

'*Perfecto. Hasta luego.*' Ale was nervous. What if she didn't come and stood him up instead? He wanted to see her again.

Reluctantly, Ale went back to meet his group to resume his guided tour. Not long to go now until he could go home and get ready to meet Alexa.

Time couldn't have gone any slower and Ale tried his best to keep his happy smile plastered on his face. That's until it was 4 o'clock and Ale had an hour to go back home, get ready and head out to meet Alexa.

5 o'clock and he was in front of her hotel. It wasn't a particularly popular one. For five stars, it played modest. And then out came Alexa, who changed into another cotton dress, wearing black flats and her hair down.

Upon spotting him, she gave a little wave and smiled before she said '*Hola.*'

'*Hola*' he replied with a grin. '*Vamos?*'

The streets were swarming with tourists and Ale wanted to get away from them. 'Come. I know a nice walking path.'

They walked towards a park and Alexa gasped when she saw all the exotic flowers and plants growing there, blooming with the help of hundreds of hummingbirds nectaring, flapping their wings over one hundred times a minute.

'This is beautiful Ale.'

'*Si.* Welcome to my country.' Alexa smiled in response.

'So what do you do, Alexa?'

'I write children's books.'

'No way! That's so cool! Have you published any?'

'Yes, some of them. With a small publication house.'

'*Que bueno.*'

'What about you?'

'I'm a tour guide.'

'Awesome. Since how long?'

'Five years.'

'I see. And are you happy?'

Ale was surprised by her question but it didn't take him long to answer.

'Yes. I love my job. I can't picture myself working anywhere else. Why? Do you not like your job?'

'I do. But I don't love it, you know?'

'Maybe you should find something you love?'

She smiled and looked up at him. 'Maybe I will. How old are you, Ale?'

'How old do you think I am?' I know I look young.'

'Maybe, but not THAT young! So you've been working as a guide for five years, right? I'd say between 25 and 27 years old.'

'I'm 27.'

'Ha! See? I'm good at this.'

He smiled. 'Yes. You're a smart cookie.' She slapped his arm playfully.

'What about you?'

'Much older.'

'Very funny.'

'No seriously.'

'Okay. 30?'

'More.'

'32?'

'Bingo.'

'Come on! That's not that much older!'

'I didn't mean it like that. It's just that...' She paused. Ale noticed she looked a bit emotional. He was about to reach out for her hand until she spoke again.

'I mean, it's like, there's less room for mistakes, you know?' Ale felt there was more to this but decided not to intrude.

A man walked past, looking at them curiously. Perhaps in this country they seemed like an unlikely pair. The three of them exchanged looks and smiles, when finally the man said *'Hola'* and the two of Ale replied simultaneously *'Hola.'*

Alexa waited till the man was out of earshot to turn to Ale and ask 'Did you see all the bling-bling around the man's neck?'

'Haha! Yeah! I know. Like Daddy Yankee!'

'Yeah, exactly!'

They laughed, noticing their similar humour. And then they talked and talked for hours about travels, love, hope.

It was getting late and Alexa needed to head back to her hotel. Ale seemed upset but understood. They walked past the exotic flowers again, the trees, the birds, when finally they reached Alexa's hotel.

They stood there for what seemed like an eternity, looking at each other.

'So...' said Alexa. 'This is it.'

Ale came closer and took her in his arms for a long, tight hug. Alexa let herself go into them. She too started feeling upset, wondering if the universe would ever reunite again one day. Ale released her, looked at her again and kissed her forehead.

'*Me hiciste el día, Alexa.*'

'*Gracias, Ale. Por todo.*'

She was about to walk into the lobby when she turned around, hoping he was still there. He was.

'Hey Ale?'

'*Si?*'

'I never asked. What's your full name?'

He smiled before answering 'Alejandro'.

'*Encantada*' she answered with a smile.

He gave a slow smile before answering, '*Mucho gusto.*'

WISHES BEFORE MIDNIGHT

It's a damp, dark, lonely night
Empty doorways and quiet whispers.

I push the sleeve off my hand;
There's five minutes left before midnight.
In this cold and hollow night,
Wishes of hope are held tightly in my hand.

I will confess and blow my wishes before midnight,
Before I hear the twelve bells and the clock glows bright.

Songs of hope when all is in despair,
Chances at love when all sparks are thought dead,
Poets to guide us when all has been thought and said.

Fifty seconds left before midnight,
I'll dream of holding clovers and coppers in my hand.

I wonder, are wishes what bind our fate and chance?

Well all I know is that I heard the twelve bells,
And my wishes have blown in the misty night.

© Chisa Togo

THE ACE

I was out of school and off to college
A chance to be cool and rock the stage
And then there she came, like a queen on her carriage
I longed to be near her, but I was out of courage

Her friends in the known made me feel out of place
But she was different with her smile and warm embrace
I thought maybe there was hope but I was just another face
I did all I could, but I was always last in the race

Countless times I walked by her without a trace
While she got all the fame and the grace
She'd be walking like she was the best, the ace
But did she love the limelight and the chase?

Her supporter to the core, but apparently invisible
I listened to her every word, each syllable so irresistible
As for me, was I so unoriginal, so pitiful?

Mother, I thought the distorted was beautiful?

Pour mes lecteurs francophones

© Abby Mansfield

DERRIÈRE L'HABIT

Un jour je l'ai suivi à travers savanes et déserts
Et Ciel sait comment il y a eu un changement dans l'air.

C'est cette marche, cette couronne, d'or et de pierres.

Derrière le masque pailleté de mystère,
Sa vie n'est plus poussière
Elle est couverte de belles choses, si délicieusement enrobées.

Derrière l'habit,
Elle n'est plus femme ordinaire
Elle ne fait plus partie du peuple populaire.

Derrière le visage voilé,
Elle s'y trouve dans un monde bien plus éloigné.

Un monde où les citoyens sont perdus dans l'imaginaire
Leurs mots et leurs poèmes honorés sous mers et sur terre.

Créatures magiques, personnages mythiques,
Ici le monde tourne sur un sens poétique.

Derrière l'habit, elle se réfugie dans sa forêt de cèdres
Silencieuse sous un arbre, elle lit ses arts littéraires.

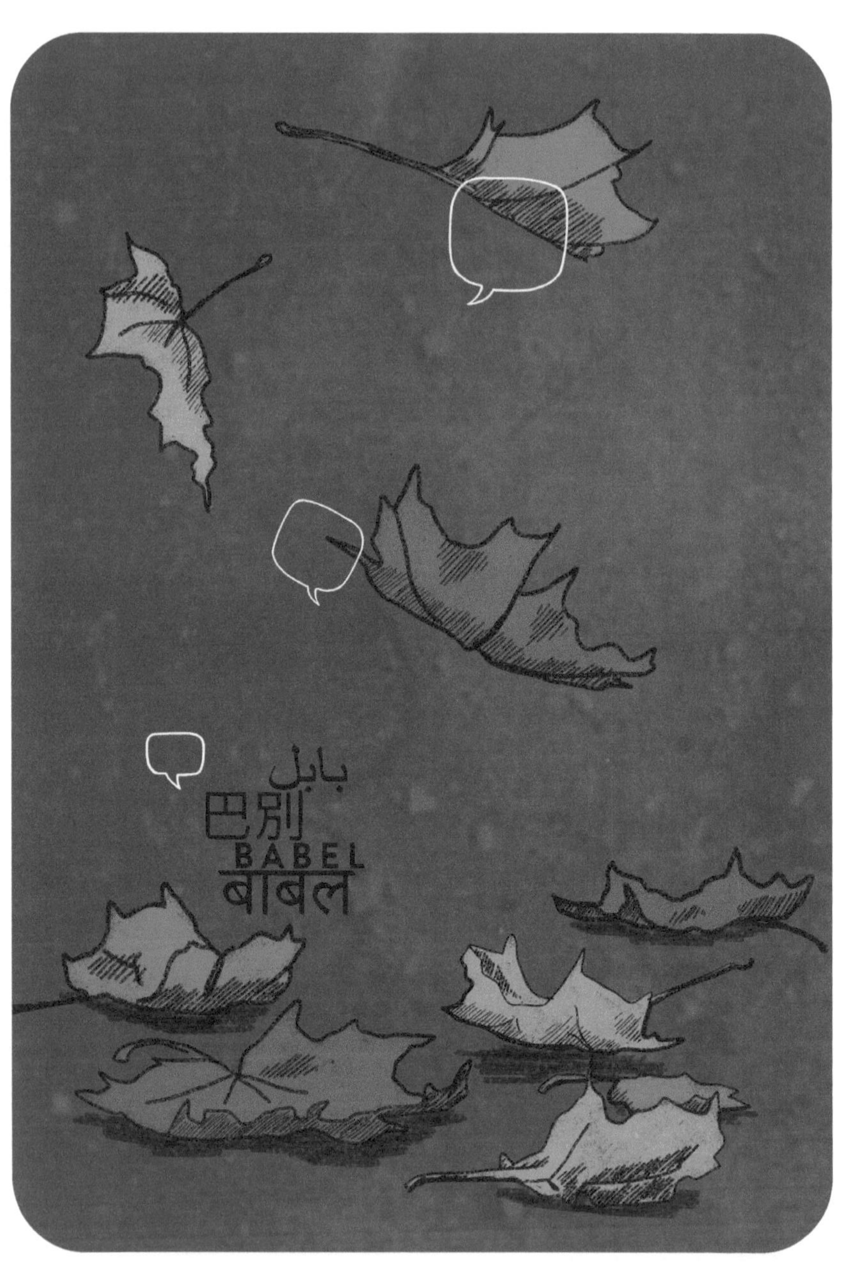

© Divya Venkatesh

SUR LE BORD DE MON BALCON

Penchés sur le bord de mon balcon,
nous matons les autres, nous jouons aux espions
car cette pastelle de couleurs nous dit que
c'est l'heure de saluer cette grande saison.

Les arbres perdent leurs feuilles, quant à nous,
nous perdons compréhension
Mes amis, à comprendre que c'est cause d'envie de l'autre
et d'expression.
Malgré poétique, elle est ruinée par une mauvaise traduction.

Ainsi pardonne-moi par avance pour mon inclination
À monter sur le carousel de sottise et d'illusion.
C'est dur de nier que la vie est bien plus belle
quand elle est enrobée d'imagination.

Je pourrais accuser les politiciens, les foutues élections
mais à quoi ça sert quand cela ne fait que répétition?

Nos souhaits sont juste des délires
Nos votes des mots à trier et à relire.
C'est vrai, c'est juste un cycle
après le froid, poussent les bourgeons
Et vers le dixième mois, nous ramassons ces tâches
de carmins et de marrons,
des canapés sur mon balcon.

CHAGRIN SUCRÉ

L'adage dit que le temps guérit
Pourtant trois cent soixante-cinq jours ne lui paraissaient pas assez
En fait ils ont suffi pour avoir été remplacée
Les nouvelles lui ont coupé et lui ont gardé blessée.

Son masque et son visage en soie dorée;
Maquillage d'un faux sourire et d'un chagrin sucré.

Elle se croyait si forte, capable de délacer
D'oublier et de courir en liberté
Mais sa vie continue avec des souvenirs cloués.

Oui le loup du passé l'a rattrapé et l'a mordu
Il lui a arraché ses sens et lui a laissé son coeur tordu.

« Sage comme une image » lui a averti l'Éducation
Celui qui lui a mené à un départ sans confession.
Une si forte imagination, mais pas assez pour une révolution.

Des promesses à Discipline, alors ses yeux lui suivaient en silence
Discrète et subtile, sur la pointe des pieds elle danse.
Ironie et tristesse qu'ils partageaient le même souhait,
Ainsi elle baisse sa tête pour se plonger,
Dans son chagrin sucré, là où elle souhaite se réfugier.

HOMME DE SOLITUDE

En haut d'une colline, vue sur une vallée abandonnée
Là j'aperçois que je suis un loup, un homme de solitude
Moment de contemplation, comment à quoi sert d'être seul,
à quoi sert l'altitude?
Je suis maître de mon monologue
Quand j'aurais pu la joindre dans son dialogue

Courageuse et la couronne de son père
Affectueuse et l'amie de sa mère
Elle était la condamnée des sourires sur mes lèvres
La chasseuse de mes nuits et de mes rêves

Dieu comment elle assemblait les créatures du désert
Quant à moi, mes mots partaient de travers
Je suis juste un homme de solitude, simple, sans tune, ordinaire

Un soir arrosé de larmes, elle me dit;
"Nous sommes les deux des apprentis
Mais regarde ce que nous avons pu construire;
Convertir de la poésie en une symphonie.
Je veux aimer et je veux bâtir."

Ses battements de coeur résonnaient dans mon désert
Mais ses mots, ses promets, étaient-ils sincères?
Un jour à l'aube quand je suis parti à la chasse,
Elle se préparait pour s'enfuir.

PIERRE DE LUNE

Reflets de lumière; bleu, or et vert,
Couleurs de l'espoir, elles chantent ma prière.

Pierre de Lune, quand la lune s'absentera,
Joue de ta magie et illumine-moi.

Parce qu'un jour l'obscurité s'imposera,
Et sans doute mon humour de joie m'y échappera.
Mais ta lumière est dont ce que j'aurai besoin,
Ton calme, ta couleur, comme tu me fera du bien.

Je te fais confiance,
Surtout à ta brillance.
Et quand je te porte, j'y crois,
A l'amour, au progrès, que l'homme peut être bien.

L'hiver enlève les pétales et il fatigue les branches,
De pire le froid est là et il toque déjà fort sur ma porte.

Pierre de Lune, je t'en supplie,
Aide-moi et joue de ta magie.

Fayruz Mandil is a Swiss-born Sudanese creative writer and the author of her first anthology, *'The Girl Dressed in Masquerade: An Anthology of Poems in French and English'*.

She is currently based in Rome, Italy, where she teaches English literature at secondary school level.

www.etsy.com/shop/FayruzMandil

ILLUSTRATORS

Ada Basford, Australia and Finland

Marie Kolly, Switzerland - @marie_kolly_

Fayruz Mandil, Switzerland and Sudan -   @wishesbeforemidnight

Abby Mansfield, United Kingdom -   @abbymansfieldart

Lauren Papot, United States -   @laurenpapot

Nina Taniguchi, Japan

Chisa Togo, Japan

Divya Venkatesh, India and Switzerland -   @divyaani

www.ingramcontent.com/pod-product-compliance
Lightning Source LLC
LaVergne TN
LVHW051455180726
843512LV00001B/46